BRIDGING HEARTS

Understanding, Strengthening, and Sustaining a Marriage

By

Grace Akinpetide, Ph.D., MABTS

Copyright Statement

Dedication

This book is dedicated to every couple who walks the path of marriage - a journey filled with love, learning, and growth. It is for those who have braved the storms of relationship struggles, who have sought to understand each other deeper, and who have committed to building a life together.

To the individuals who strive to balance personal growth with the demands of nurturing a family, your resilience and dedication are the backbone of every strong marriage. This book is a tribute to your journey, a recognition of the challenges you face, and an acknowledgment of the love that keeps you united.

May "Bridging Hearts" serve as a beacon of hope, a source of strength, and a companion in your journey to create a bond that is not only enduring but also enriching. May it remind you that in the intricate dance of marriage, every step taken together is a step towards a deeper understanding and a stronger bond.

Acknowledgment

I sincerely thank the Almighty God, the divine architect of all marriages. Your wisdom, grace, and boundless love are the foundation for every godly marriage. Thank You for guiding my pen and infusing these pages with Your divine wisdom.

May God's grace shine upon every married couple seeking to nurture a godly marriage. May this book be a beacon of His light and a reminder that you can build a lasting, fulfilling, and God-centered union with faith, devotion, and love.

Table of Content

Preface

In the intricate tapestry of human existence, there is perhaps no journey more profound and yet perilous than the quest for love and connection. The bonds we form, the vows we exchange, and the hearts we unite in the sacred institution of marriage stand as a testament to our deepest desires, our highest aspirations, and our unyielding hope for a love that can weather life's storms. But, as the saying goes, the path to true love is never a smooth one. In the course of our lives, we inevitably encounter situations where relationships strain, trust is broken, and bridges are burned. It is within these moments of adversity that we must summon the strength to mend what is torn, to heal what is broken, and to rekindle the flames of love that first brought two hearts together.

"Bridging Hearts: Understanding, Strengthening, and Sustaining Marriage" is a profound exploration of the multifaceted journey that is marriage, a voyage through the depths of the human heart, and a quest to not only salvage but to fortify the most intimate of partnerships. This is a book that seeks to be a guiding light, a compassionate confidant, and an unwavering source of wisdom in the tumultuous seas of matrimony.

In the first part of our journey, we delve into the foundations of a healthy marriage. We contemplate marriage not as a mere contract but as a divine union blessed by God Himself. We trace the historical tapestry of relationships, seeking wisdom from the past while defining relationships in the ever-evolving modern world. And, at the heart of it all, we explore the pivotal role of love in nurturing a marriage that is not only surviving but thriving.

From there, we embark on a deep dive into the nurturing of intimacy in relationships. Physical and emotional intimacy, the essential building blocks of any strong union, takes center stage. We dissect the importance of sexual intimacy, and, just as crucially, we explore new dimensions of connection and discuss how to overcome common intimacy issues that can strain even the strongest of bonds.

Our journey doesn't stop at the confines of marital connection; it extends to the profound relationship between parents and children. The timeless question of how to raise godly offspring, build bonds that stand the test of time, and instill values and morals in the hearts of the next generation becomes our focus.

Yet, as in any journey, the path is not without its obstacles. In the second part of our book, we turn our gaze towards the recognition and addressing of relationship struggles. We identify common issues and challenges faced by couples, analyze the impact of external factors, and uncover the telltale signs of a marriage in distress.

At the heart of these struggles, we confront a formidable adversary: narcissism. In a world where self-centeredness and ego often threaten the sanctity of marriage, we define and examine narcissistic behaviors. We help you recognize the subtle traits of narcissism in a partner and navigate the treacherous waters of narcissistic abuse. We discuss the red flags and warning signs, as well as the profound impact on both the spouse and the marriage itself.

Finally, we offer a lifeline to those who find themselves ensnared in the grip of narcissistic abuse. The healing process, coping strategies for dealing with a narcissistic partner, and the challenging road to recovery are all laid bare, along with insights into why overcoming narcissistic abuse trauma can be a long and arduous journey.

As we reach the reflection and conclusion of our odyssey, we invite you to pause, look back on your own marriage, and consider the lessons and insights you've gained. With our final thoughts and takeaways, we hope to leave you with the tools, wisdom, and inspiration needed to bridge the hearts that matter most in your life. For love is a journey, and "Bridging Hearts" is your compass, your guide, and your unwavering companion along the way.

"Marriage, the remarkable bridge that unites two hearts,

thrives when built on understanding, fortified by strength, and sustained with unshakable love!"

Grace Akinpetide, Ph.D., MABTS

PART 1: Foundations of a Healthy Marriage

CHAPTER ONE

Marriage as a Divine Union

1.1   Marriage: A Union Blessed by God

❖ *The Existence of Marriage*

In the sacred tapestry of human existence, there exists a profound and divine institution - marriage. This union, ordained by the Creator, is a testament to the boundless love and wisdom that permeates the very fabric of our existence. From the very beginning in the book of Genesis, the Scriptures resound with the declaration that God said, "It is not good for man to be alone" (Genesis 2:18). Thus, in His infinite wisdom, He created Eve, the first woman, to be a companion, a helper, and a partner for Adam. This act of divine creation set the stage for the institution of marriage, illustrating that it is part of God's grand design for humanity.

In the book of Genesis, we find a description of the first wedding ceremony in the Garden of Eden. "Therefore, a man shall leave his father and mother and be joined to his wife, and they shall become one flesh" (Genesis 2:24). This verse underscores the profound spiritual significance of the marital union, emphasizing the leaving of one's familial bonds and the establishment of a new, sacred bond between a man and a woman.

This union, often referred to as the "one-flesh" relationship, symbolizes the deep and inseparable connection between a husband and wife. It is a bond that transcends the physical and emotional aspects of human existence, reaching into the spiritual realm. In this sacred union, two individuals come together to form a new entity, a partnership that reflects the unity of God's love and His plan for humanity.

❖ *A Sacred Covenant*

Marriage is often referred to as a sacred covenant, and this designation is not without reason. A covenant, in the biblical sense, is a solemn agreement between two parties that carries with it profound moral and spiritual implications. When two individuals come together in marriage, they are not only entering into a legal and social contract, but they are also entering into a spiritual covenant before God.

In the same way that God made covenants with His people throughout the Bible, such as the covenant with Noah, Abraham, and Moses, marriage represents a covenant between a man and a woman and ultimately with God. It is a commitment to love, honor, and cherish one another, in sickness and in health, for richer or poorer, until death do us part. This commitment is not to be taken lightly, for it reflects the depth of love and faithfulness that God expects from His people.

❖ *A Reflection of God's Love*

Marriage is a beautiful reflection of God's love for His creation. Just as God loves His people unconditionally, marriage calls us to love one another unconditionally. It challenges us to extend grace, forgiveness, and patience to our spouses, just as God extends these qualities to us. In marriage, we learn to mirror the sacrificial love that Christ showed for His Church, loving our spouse with the same selflessness and devotion.

In Ephesians 5:25-28, the apostle Paul writes, "Husbands, love your wives, just as Christ loved the church and gave himself up for her." This verse underscores the sacrificial nature of love within marriage. It's a love that puts the needs and well-being of one's spouse above one's own desires.

1.2   The Profound Purpose of Marriage

The purpose of marriage, as ordained by God, extends far beyond the fulfillment of personal desires or societal norms. It stands as a profound vehicle through which human beings embark on a transformative journey, impacting their lives and the world around them in ways that are truly awe-inspiring.

> ➢ *Companionship and emotional support*

At its core, marriage is a celestial union that brings two souls together in an eternal bond of companionship. It provides a haven of love and understanding, where two individuals embark on a shared journey, creating a sanctuary of emotional support, affection, and a deep sense of belonging. It is in this union that people find solace in their partner's presence, navigating the ebb and flow of life hand in hand.

> ➢ *Procreation and family building*

In the grand design of creation, marriage is a vessel for procreation, a divine mandate to perpetuate life and ensure the continuation of the human race. The family unit that emerges from marriage becomes the nurturing ground for the next generation, providing a loving and stable environment for the upbringing of children. In this role, marriage plays an essential part in shaping the future of humanity.

➢ *Spiritual Growth and Mutual Transformation*

Marriage is a remarkable crucible for spiritual growth. As two people unite, they embark on a journey of self-discovery, honing their patience, compassion, and resilience. Together, they strive to become the best versions of themselves, drawing strength from one another's unwavering love and support. The challenges and triumphs encountered in marriage serve as stepping stones for personal and spiritual development, fostering a profound connection that goes beyond the earthly realm.

➢ *Societal Stability*

Marriage is not just a personal commitment; it's a cornerstone of societal stability. Strong marriages are the building blocks of a harmonious and thriving society. They provide a stable environment for the upbringing of children and foster a sense of responsibility, commitment, and shared values. A society where marriage is held in high regard is one where individuals are more likely to find security, support, and the foundation needed to pursue their dreams.

➢ *Reflection of God's Image*

Marriage is a reflection of the divine plan itself. In coming together, two individuals mirror the profound unity of God's love, serving as living testaments to the harmonious duality that exists in the universe. Through the union of two distinct souls, the divine image is manifested, and the strength of love becomes a beacon for all to witness.

1.3   Components of a Godly Marriage

A godly marriage, as described in the previous section, is a sacred covenant that reflects God's love, has profound purposes, and is a reflection of God's image. To maintain and nurture such a marriage, there are several key components:

a)   ***Faith and Spirituality:*** A godly marriage is grounded in faith and spirituality. Both partners should have a strong relationship with God and a shared spiritual foundation. This shared faith is the cornerstone that supports the marriage covenant and provides a source of guidance and strength in times of joy and hardship.

b)   ***Commitment:*** Commitment in a godly marriage means a lifelong dedication to each other, just as God's commitment to His people is unwavering. This commitment extends beyond mere promises and involves putting the needs and well-being of your spouse above your own. It's a commitment to love, honor, and cherish one another, regardless of the circumstances.

c)   ***Communication:*** Effective communication is vital in any marriage, but in a godly marriage, it is even more essential. Open and honest communication fosters understanding and helps resolve conflicts in a way that is consistent with the principles of love, grace, and forgiveness.

d)   ***Selflessness:*** A godly marriage calls for selflessness, where both partners prioritize each other's well-being. This means putting your spouse's needs ahead of your own desires and being willing to make sacrifices for the sake of the relationship.

e)   ***Love and Forgiveness:*** Godly love is unconditional and sacrificial, mirroring the love Christ has for the Church. This kind of love is characterized by patience, forgiveness, and a willingness to extend grace, just as God does for us.

While embracing the concept of forgiveness as advocated in the Bible, it is essential to exercise wisdom when confronted with individuals who repeatedly seek forgiveness without genuine repentance. Drawing inspiration from the unconditional and sacrificial love exemplified by Christ for the Church, one should be discerning about those who may exploit forgiveness as a means of manipulation, control, or gaslighting. In such instances, applying wisdom becomes imperative, recognizing the need for discernment in order to navigate complex relationships and ensure that forgiveness is not misused or taken for granted.

f)   ***Humility:*** Humility is essential in a godly marriage. It involves acknowledging one's own shortcomings and being willing to apologize and seek forgiveness when necessary. Humility fosters a spirit of reconciliation and growth.

g)   ***Prayer and Worship:*** Regular prayer and worship together can strengthen the spiritual bond between a husband and wife. It allows the couple to seek God's guidance, express gratitude, and request His blessing on their marriage.

h)   ***Shared Values and Goals:*** Partners in a godly marriage should have shared values, beliefs, and life goals. These common principles and objectives provide a strong foundation for making decisions and facing life's challenges together.

i)   ***Intimacy and Connection:*** Physical and emotional intimacy is an important component of a godly marriage. Intimacy is not just about physical affection but also about emotional connection and closeness. A healthy sexual relationship within the bounds of marriage is considered a gift from God.

A godly marriage is built on a strong foundation of faith, love, and commitment. It requires ongoing effort and a deep commitment to upholding the sacred covenant before God. By incorporating these components into their marriage, couples can nurture a relationship that reflects the divine love and purpose described in the previous section.

CHAPTER TWO

Nurturing Intimacy in Relationships

2.1   Understanding Physical and Emotional Intimacy

❖ *Defining Intimacy*

Intimacy is a multifaceted concept encompassing both physical and emotional dimensions. It is the glue that binds two people together, creating a sense of closeness and connection that goes beyond the superficial.

➤ *Physical Intimacy*

Physical intimacy involves more than just sexual activities; it encompasses all forms of physical affection, closeness, and touch between partners. This can range from holding hands, cuddling, hugging, and kissing to the most intimate of acts. The importance of physical intimacy cannot be overstated in a romantic relationship.

1)   ***Communication Through Touch:*** Physical intimacy often speaks louder than words. A simple touch on the shoulder, a warm hug, or an affectionate kiss can convey love, desire,

comfort, and security. These gestures are not just enjoyable but essential for emotional connection and bonding.

2) ***Sexual Intimacy:*** Sexual intimacy is a powerful and unique aspect of romantic relationships. It's a deeply personal expression of love and desire. Open and honest communication about sexual needs and desires is vital to maintaining a satisfying sexual connection. Explore each other's boundaries, preferences, and fantasies to deepen your sexual intimacy.

3) ***Vulnerability:*** Being physically intimate requires vulnerability. Sharing your body and desires with your partner is a profound act of trust and emotional intimacy. A strong emotional connection enhances physical intimacy, making it more fulfilling and enjoyable.

➢ *Emotional Intimacy*

Emotional intimacy is the foundation of any successful relationship. It's about opening up, being vulnerable, and connecting on a deeper level with your partner. Here are some key elements of emotional intimacy:

1) ***Effective Communication***: Being emotionally intimate means actively listening and expressing your thoughts, feelings, and fears with your partner. Open and honest communication is the key to understanding each other better.

2) ***Trust and Vulnerability:*** Trust is at the heart of emotional intimacy. It's about feeling safe enough to share your innermost thoughts and feelings without fear of judgment. Vulnerability is the willingness to be open and honest, even when it's uncomfortable.

3) ***Empathy and Support:*** Being emotionally intimate involves empathizing with your partner's feelings and providing support in times of need. Knowing that your partner has your back can strengthen the emotional bond.

4) ***Quality Time:*** Spending quality time together fosters emotional intimacy. This can be in the form of deep conversations, shared experiences, or simply being present with each other without distractions.

5) ***Shared Goals and Values:*** Having common goals and values can strengthen emotional intimacy by providing a sense of purpose and direction in your relationship.

2.2   The Role of Intimacy in Building Strong Connections

> ### ➢ *A Solid Foundation for Trust*

Intimacy serves as the bedrock upon which trust is built. When you allow someone into your physical and emotional space, you're essentially saying, "I trust you with my vulnerability." This trust forms the cornerstone of any lasting relationship. It's the belief that your partner will safeguard your innermost thoughts and feelings and that you will do the same for them.

Trust isn't just about keeping secrets; it's about relying on each other in times of need, knowing that your partner will be there for you. Trust enables you to weather the storms of life together, secure in the knowledge that you have an unwavering ally by your side. And this trust, in turn, deepens the bonds of intimacy, creating a self-reinforcing cycle of closeness and connection.

> ### *The Fertilizer for Emotional Growth*

Intimacy isn't just a static state of being; it's a dynamic force that nurtures emotional growth. In a truly intimate relationship, both partners support each other's personal development. They encourage each other to face their fears, challenge their limitations, and pursue their dreams. It's a relationship where you not only find love but also the opportunity to become the best version of yourself.

The support and encouragement found in intimate relationships can be a powerful catalyst for individual growth. When you have a partner who believes in you, who cheers you on, and who understands your inner world, it becomes easier to take risks, step out of your comfort zone, and pursue your passions. In such an environment, both partners can blossom, and their connection deepens as they witness each other's personal evolution.

2.3   The Importance of Sexual Intimacy

Sexual intimacy is a vital component of overall intimacy in a romantic relationship. It adds a unique and deeply fulfilling dimension to the connection between two individuals. While it's not the sole basis of a strong partnership, sexual intimacy plays a crucial role in enhancing emotional bonds and fostering a healthy, robust relationship. In this section, we explore the importance of sexual intimacy and its impact on romantic connections.

> ### *A Bond Unlike Any Other*

Sexual intimacy creates a bond between partners that is unlike any other. It's a way to express desire, passion, and love in a physical form. The act of making love allows individuals to connect on a deeply primal level, transcending words and emotions. It can be a profound and transcendent experience, fostering a sense of unity and oneness with your partner.

This physical closeness releases a flood of neurochemicals in the brain, including oxytocin and dopamine, which promote feelings of love, attachment, and pleasure. It's a biological mechanism that reinforces the emotional connection between partners. Moreover, it's a means of non-verbal communication, allowing partners to convey their affection and desire in a way that words alone can't replicate.

➤ *Enhancing Emotional Intimacy*

Sexual intimacy and emotional intimacy are intertwined; they reinforce and complement each other. When a couple experiences a healthy and satisfying sexual connection, it often leads to a deeper emotional bond. Sharing these intimate moments fosters trust, vulnerability, and open communication, which are essential elements of emotional intimacy.

Furthermore, it provides a safe space for partners to be their authentic selves, free from judgment or fear. When individuals feel desired and accepted in their most vulnerable state, it strengthens the foundation of emotional intimacy. It's a reminder that their partner loves and desires them not just for their physical attributes but for who they are as a whole person.

➤ *Fulfilling the Needs of Both Partners*

In a romantic relationship, it's essential to recognize that different individuals have varying levels of sexual desire and needs. The key to a successful sexual connection is open and honest communication. Understanding and respecting each other's desires, boundaries, and preferences are crucial to maintaining a healthy and satisfying sexual relationship.

Meeting the sexual needs of both partners contributes to a sense of equity and satisfaction within the relationship. It ensures that both individuals feel valued and loved, fostering a harmonious and balanced connection. While sexual compatibility is not the sole determinant of a successful relationship, it can be a contributing factor to its overall health and happiness.

Sexual intimacy is a vital part of a romantic relationship that enhances emotional bonds, fosters closeness and contributes to overall satisfaction and happiness. It's a unique and beautiful way for partners to connect on a physical and emotional level, deepening their love and understanding of each other. To maintain a thriving and robust partnership, it's important to prioritize open communication and mutual understanding when it comes to sexual intimacy.

2.4   Exploring New Dimensions of Intimacy

Intimacy is a dynamic force that evolves over time. While physical, emotional, and sexual intimacy are foundational components of any relationship, there are myriad other dimensions of intimacy that can further enrich and strengthen the connections between individuals.

1)   Intellectual Intimacy

Intellectual intimacy is the connection that arises when two individuals share their thoughts, ideas, and knowledge with one another. It's the spark that ignites during meaningful conversations and debates. When partners engage in stimulating intellectual discussions, they not only expand their own horizons but also create a bond built on shared values and a mutual understanding of the world. Intellectual intimacy invites partners to learn from each other, challenge each other's perspectives, and grow together intellectually.

2)   *Spiritual Intimacy*

Spiritual intimacy is the connection formed when individuals explore and share their beliefs, values, and philosophies of life. It's not limited to religious affiliations; it can encompass a wide range of spiritual or philosophical outlooks. When partners engage in spiritual discussions, rituals, or practices, they connect on a profound level, finding common ground in the way they seek purpose, meaning, and connection in the universe. Spiritual intimacy deepens the sense of unity and shared purpose in a relationship.

3)   *Recreational Intimacy*

Recreational intimacy is about sharing and enjoying hobbies, activities, and adventures with your partner. It can be as simple as cooking together, going for a hike, or pursuing a shared interest like dancing or painting. Engaging in recreational activities as a couple strengthens the bond through shared experiences, laughter, and the joy of creating memories together. Recreational intimacy encourages couples to enjoy life and have fun as a team.

4)   *Digital Intimacy*

In the age of technology, digital intimacy has become increasingly important. It encompasses the ways partners connect and communicate through digital channels, such as texting, video calls, and social media. Sharing your daily life, thoughts, and emotions with your partner online can create a sense of constant connection and closeness, even when physically apart. It's a way to bridge the gap in long-distance relationships and maintain a sense of togetherness.

5)   Experiential Intimacy

Experiential intimacy is all about sharing unique and memorable experiences with your partner. It can be a trip to a foreign country, attending a concert, or trying something new together, like skydiving or learning to cook a new cuisine. These shared adventures create lasting memories and deepen the emotional connection between partners. They remind couples of the excitement and vitality they bring into each other's lives.

6)   Financial Intimacy

Financial intimacy involves open and transparent communication about money matters. It's about setting financial goals together, budgeting as a team, and making financial decisions that align with both partners' values and aspirations. Financial intimacy helps avoid conflicts related to money and ensures that both partners are on the same page when it comes to their financial future.

Relationships are not one-dimensional, and intimacy can take on many forms. Exploring these new dimensions of intimacy offers opportunities to strengthen the bond between partners and foster deeper connections. By embracing intellectual, spiritual, recreational, digital, experiential, and financial intimacy, couples can enhance their relationship in ways that are unique and meaningful to them, leading to a richer, more fulfilling partnership.

2.5　Overcoming Common Intimacy Issues

While intimacy is a beautiful and essential aspect of human relationships, it's not without its challenges. Many couples encounter common intimacy issues that can strain their connections. However, these issues are not insurmountable. Below are the common intimacy issues and offer strategies to overcome them, ensuring that your relationships remain strong and fulfilling.

❖ *Communication Barriers*

One of the most prevalent intimacy issues is a lack of effective communication. This can manifest as misunderstandings, misinterpretations, or unspoken desires and concerns. To overcome communication barriers, it's essential to:

1) *Practice active listening:* Pay close attention to your partner when they speak. Show empathy and understanding by asking questions and seeking clarification.

2) *Express yourself honestly:* Be open and transparent about your thoughts and feelings. Avoid bottling up emotions or avoiding difficult conversations.

3) *Use "I" statements:* Phrase your concerns or desires in a way that focuses on your feelings and experiences rather than making accusatory statements.

❖ *Trust Issues*

Trust is the foundation of intimacy, and when it's compromised, intimacy can suffer. Trust issues may stem from past betrayals, insecurities, or fears. To rebuild trust, consider:

1) ***Open conversations:*** Discuss your concerns with your partner, sharing how the breach of trust affected you and what can be done to rebuild it.

2) ***Consistency:*** Demonstrate trustworthiness through your actions over time, showing your partner that they can rely on you.

❖ *Emotional Distance*

Sometimes, couples experience emotional distance, where they feel disconnected or out of sync. To bridge this gap and restore emotional intimacy, you can:

1) ***Reconnect with shared activities:*** Rekindle the flame by revisiting activities or hobbies that initially brought you closer.

2) ***Plan quality time:*** Set aside dedicated time for each other, free from distractions, where you can focus on rebuilding your emotional connection.

3) ***Seek professional guidance:*** In cases of persistent emotional distance, consider therapy to identify underlying issues and develop strategies to address them.

❖ *Mismatched Sexual Desire*

Sexual intimacy mismatches are common, with one partner desiring more or less sex than the other. To address this issue:

1) ***Open dialogue:*** Talk about your desires, boundaries, and fantasies with your partner. Honesty is crucial to finding a compromise.

2) ***Compromise:*** Find a balance that both partners are comfortable with, whether it means increasing the frequency or adjusting expectations.

3) ***Professional help:*** In some cases, consulting a sex therapist can provide valuable insights and strategies to resolve sexual intimacy issues.

❖ *Past Traumas*

Past traumas can cast a shadow over intimacy, causing emotional wounds and inhibitions. To overcome the impact of past traumas:

1) ***Patience and support:*** Be understanding and patient with your partner. Create a safe space where they can open up about their past without judgment.

2) ***Seek therapy:*** Trauma therapy or counseling can help individuals work through their past experiences and develop coping strategies.

3) ***Educate yourself:*** Understanding the effects of trauma can help you support your partner better and navigate intimacy with sensitivity.

❖ *External Stressors*

Life's challenges, such as work, financial issues, and family problems, can place strain on relationships. To overcome external stressors:

1) ***Collaboration:*** Approach these challenges as a team, supporting each other through difficult times and finding solutions together.

2) ***Regular check-ins:*** Ensure that you regularly communicate about how these stressors affect your relationship and make adjustments as needed.

3) ***Self-care:*** Taking care of your mental and emotional well-being is essential. Engage in activities that help you manage stress, both individually and as a couple.

Intimacy issues are a common part of most relationships, but with the right strategies and a commitment to open and honest communication, they can be addressed and resolved. By actively working on these challenges, couples can strengthen their bonds, ensuring that intimacy remains a vibrant and essential aspect of their connection. Remember, it's the effort and willingness to address these issues that can lead to deeper and more fulfilling relationships.

(CHAPTER THREE)

Parent-Child Relationships

Parent-child relationships are among the most profound and influential connections one can experience. The bonds formed between parents and their children have a lasting impact on a child's development, well-being, and future relationships. In this chapter, we delve into the complexities and joys of nurturing godly offspring, building strong parent-child bonds, and instilling values and morals in your children.

3.1   Nurturing Godly Offspring

❖ *The Divine Responsibility*

Nurturing godly offspring is a sacred responsibility for many parents. While this concept may be rooted in religious or spiritual beliefs, it is fundamentally about raising children with a strong moral and ethical foundation. It involves guiding them on a path of integrity, compassion, and faith, whatever your beliefs may be. Key aspects of nurturing godly offspring include:

1) ***Teaching values:*** Imparting a set of core values that encompass honesty, kindness, empathy, and a sense of purpose.

2) ***Leading by example:*** Demonstrating the values and principles you wish to instill in your children through your own actions and behavior.

3) ***Spiritual guidance***: If applicable, providing spiritual and religious teachings that align with your family's beliefs.

4) ***Promoting moral growth:*** Encouraging critical thinking and ethical decision-making in your children as they grow and face increasingly complex moral dilemmas.

❖ *The Role of Love and Respect*

Love and respect are the cornerstones of nurturing godly offspring. Children need to feel unconditionally loved and respected by their parents to grow into morally upright individuals. Love provides the emotional security and support that allows children to develop their sense of self-worth. Respect, on the other hand, teaches them to value others and their opinions.

It's essential to strike a balance between nurturing and disciplining. Discipline, when carried out with love and respect, can reinforce the values and morals you're trying to impart. This approach fosters an environment where children are more likely to learn from their mistakes and make better choices in the future.

3.2   Building Strong Parent-Child Bonds

❖ *The Importance of Connection*

A strong parent-child bond is the foundation of a healthy relationship. It's this bond that provides children with a sense of safety and trust, allowing them to explore the world with confidence. Here are some key strategies for building strong parent-child bonds:

a) ***Quality time:*** Spend time with your children engaged in activities they enjoy. Whether it's playing, reading, or simply talking, these moments create lasting connections.

b) ***Active listening:*** Pay close attention to your child's thoughts and feelings, demonstrating empathy and understanding.

c) ***Unconditional love:*** Ensure your children know that your love for them is unwavering, regardless of their actions or behavior.

d) ***Encouragement and support:*** Foster a sense of self-worth and confidence by celebrating your child's achievements and offering guidance during challenges.

❖ *Communication and Trust*

Open and honest communication is the bedrock of a strong parent-child bond. Trust is built upon the foundation of effective communication. It's important to create an environment where your child feels safe discussing their thoughts, fears, and aspirations. Encourage them to share their concerns and questions with you, knowing that they can trust your guidance and support.

3.3 Instilling Values and Morals in Your Children

❖ *Leading by Example*

Children often learn values and morals through observation and emulation. As parents, your actions and behavior play a significant role in instilling these principles in your children. Here's how you can lead by example:

1) ***Consistency:*** Be consistent in demonstrating the values and morals you want to instill in your children. They learn by observing your behavior over time.

2) ***Teachable moments:*** Take advantage of everyday situations to discuss values and morals. Use real-life examples to illustrate your teachings.

3) ***Apologize when necessary:*** If you make a mistake or act in a way that contradicts the values you're teaching, be willing to apologize and explain your actions.

4) ***Encourage critical thinking:*** Encourage your children to think for themselves, ask questions, and consider the implications of their actions.

❖ *Sharing Stories and Narratives*

Stories and narratives have long been used as powerful tools for imparting values and morals. Share stories, fables, or parables that carry moral lessons with your children. Discuss the characters' choices and their consequences, helping your children understand the importance of making ethical decisions.

❖ *Encourage Ethical Decision-Making*

Teaching children to make ethical decisions involves:

1) ***Guided reasoning:*** Help your children think through moral dilemmas by asking open-ended questions that encourage them to consider the implications of their choices.

2) ***Consequences:*** Discuss the potential consequences of different choices and how they might affect others.

3) ***Empathy:*** Encourage your children to put themselves in others' shoes to better understand how their actions impact those around them.

4) ***Respect for diversity:*** Teach your children to respect and appreciate differences in culture, belief, and perspective.

Nurturing godly offspring, building strong parent-child bonds, and instilling values and morals in your children are essential aspects of effective parenting. It's a journey that requires love, patience, and continuous effort. By fostering these connections and teaching essential values, parents can raise children who not only carry these values into their own lives but also contribute positively to their communities and the world.

PART 2: Recognizing and Addressing Relationship Struggles

(CHAPTER FOUR)

Recognizing Struggles in Marriage

Marriage is a journey filled with joy, love, and connection, but it's not without its challenges. In this chapter, we'll explore the common issues and challenges that couples often face, as well as the impact of external factors on their relationships. We'll also delve into the signs that may indicate a struggling marriage, helping couples to identify areas in need of attention and improvement.

4.1 Identifying Common Issues and Challenges

❖ *Communication Breakdown*

One of the most prevalent issues in marriage is a breakdown in communication. This may manifest as miscommunication, misunderstandings, or a lack of effective dialogue. When couples fail to communicate their needs, feelings, and concerns, it can lead to resentment, frustration, and emotional distance.

❖ *Conflict and Resentment*

All couples encounter conflicts, but how they handle them can significantly impact their relationship. Unresolved conflicts can lead to built-up resentment, which can erode the foundation of a marriage over time. Learning healthy conflict resolution techniques is essential for maintaining a strong relationship.

❖ *Emotional Distance*

Married couples may find themselves feeling emotionally distant from each other. This can result from various factors, including life stressors, differing priorities, or a lack of quality time together. Emotional distance can lead to a sense of disconnection and unhappiness in the marriage.

❖ *Intimacy Issues*

Sexual and emotional intimacy can become problematic in a marriage. Changes in sexual desire, life stressors, or emotional barriers can all contribute to intimacy issues. Addressing these issues is crucial for maintaining a healthy and fulfilling marriage.

❖ *Financial Struggles*

Financial problems, such as debt, differing spending habits, or unemployment, can place stress on a marriage. Disagreements about money can lead to tension and conflicts within the relationship.

4.2   Analyzing the Impact of External Factors

➢ *Work and Career*

External factors like demanding careers, long work hours, and job-related stress can take a toll on a marriage. Balancing work and personal life is essential to prevent these external factors from negatively affecting the relationship.

➢ *Family and In-Laws*

Family dynamics and relationships with in-laws can have a significant impact on a marriage. Struggles with extended family members, boundary issues, and conflicting expectations can create stress and conflicts within the marriage.

➢ *Health and Illness*

Health-related challenges, whether one partner's illness or the health of a child, can add emotional and practical strains to a marriage. Coping with these challenges together is vital for maintaining the relationship's strength.

➢ *External Stressors*

General life stressors, such as financial problems, housing issues, or societal pressures, can affect a marriage. The way a couple handles external stressors can determine the impact on their relationship.

4.3   Signs of a Struggling Marriage

➢ *Increased Arguments*

Frequent and escalating arguments or conflicts can be a clear sign that a marriage is struggling. If small disagreements turn into major disputes regularly, it may indicate deeper issues.

➢ *Emotional Disconnection*

Emotional disconnection, where partners feel distant, indifferent, or no longer share their inner worlds with each other, is a red flag. An emotional connection is the lifeblood of a healthy marriage.

➢ *Decreased Intimacy*

A significant drop in sexual intimacy or emotional intimacy can signal problems within the relationship. It's essential to address and work on rebuilding intimacy if it's waning.

➢ *Escapism or Avoidance*

If one or both partners are seeking escapism through activities like excessive work, socializing, or spending time online, it may be a sign that they are avoiding issues within the marriage.

➢ *Contemplation of Separation or Divorce*

When one or both partners start contemplating separation or divorce, it's a clear indication that the marriage is facing severe challenges. At this point, seeking professional help is often advisable.

Recognizing and addressing the struggles in a marriage is essential for maintaining a healthy and fulfilling partnership. By identifying common issues, understanding the impact of external factors, and being vigilant about signs of a struggling marriage, couples can take proactive steps to address challenges, seek support, and work together to strengthen their relationship.

Understanding Narcissism in Marriage

Narcissism can have a profound impact on a marriage, affecting not only the narcissistic partner but also the spouse. In this chapter, we will delve into the definition and types of narcissistic behaviors, how to recognize narcissistic traits in a partner, the red flags and warning signs, and the impact of narcissism on the spouse and the marriage as a whole.

5.1 Definition and Types of Narcissistic Behaviors

❖ *Understanding Narcissism*

Narcissism is a personality trait characterized by a strong need for admiration, a lack of empathy, and an inflated sense of self-importance. While some degree of narcissism is common in most people, narcissistic personality disorder (NPD) represents a more extreme and pervasive form of this trait. Narcissistic behaviors can manifest in various ways, making it essential to distinguish between healthy self-confidence and problematic narcissism.

❖ *Types of Narcissistic Behaviors*

1) ***Grandiose Narcissism:*** Individuals with grandiose narcissism exhibit an exaggerated sense of self-importance, a constant need for attention and admiration, and a tendency to exploit others for personal gain.

2) ***Communal Narcissism:*** Some narcissists portray themselves as selfless and caring, emphasizing their willingness to help others. However, this is often a facade, serving their need for admiration.

It's important to note that narcissistic behaviors can manifest in various ways, and the types mentioned above are just a couple of examples. The mental health field recognizes a spectrum of narcissistic traits, and an individual may exhibit a combination of these traits. Additionally, the manifestation of narcissistic behaviors can vary in intensity, with some individuals displaying more severe traits associated with narcissistic personality disorder. Understanding these nuances can contribute to a more comprehensive understanding of narcissism and its impact on individuals and relationships.

5.2   Recognizing Narcissistic Traits in a Partner

❖ *Signs of Narcissistic Traits*

Recognizing narcissistic traits in a partner can be challenging, as they often vary in intensity and presentation. Some common signs include:

a)   A strong need for constant admiration and validation.

b)   A lack of empathy and an inability to consider others' feelings.

c)   A sense of entitlement and an expectation of special treatment.

d)   Manipulative or controlling behaviors.

e)   An inclination to exploit others for personal gain.

5.3   Red Flags and Warning Signs

❖ *Red Flags of Narcissism*

While it's essential to approach the recognition of narcissistic traits with sensitivity and caution, some red flags may indicate the presence of problematic narcissism in a partner:

1) ***Manipulative behavior:*** If your partner habitually manipulates situations or people to their advantage and is often dishonest or deceitful, this is a significant warning sign.

2) ***Inflated ego:*** A partner with an unrelenting belief in their superiority and importance, coupled with a disregard for your needs and feelings, may exhibit narcissistic behaviors.

3) ***Frequent conflicts and blame:*** A pattern of constant conflict, with your partner avoiding accountability for their actions and blaming you or others, can be indicative of narcissism.

5.4 Impact on the Spouse and Marriage

❖ *The Impact of Narcissism on the Spouse*

Being in a relationship with a narcissistic partner can have a profound emotional and psychological impact on the spouse. Common effects may include:

1) ***Low self-esteem:*** Constant criticism and invalidation from a narcissistic partner can erode the self-esteem and self-worth of the spouse.

2) ***Emotional distress:*** Spouses of narcissists often experience heightened stress, anxiety, and depression due to frequent conflicts and emotional manipulation.

3) ***Isolation:*** Narcissistic partners may isolate their spouse from friends and family, making the spouse more dependent on the narcissist.

4) ***Loss of personal identity:*** The spouse may gradually lose their sense of self as they cater to the narcissistic partner's needs and demands.

❖ *The Impact on the Marriage*

Narcissism can have a detrimental impact on the marriage as well:

1) ***High conflict:*** Marriages involving a narcissistic partner often experience frequent conflicts, power struggles, and communication breakdowns.

2)   ***Lack of emotional intimacy:*** Narcissists may struggle to offer emotional support, resulting in a lack of emotional intimacy in the marriage.

3)   ***Stress and tension:*** The constant need for validation and admiration can create a tense and stressful atmosphere in the marriage.

4)   ***Risk of dissolution:*** Narcissistic behaviors can put the marriage at risk, with a higher likelihood of separation or divorce if the issues are not addressed.

Understanding narcissism in marriage is a complex and challenging endeavor. Recognizing narcissistic traits, red flags, and warning signs is the first step in addressing the issue. In the following chapters, we will explore strategies for coping with a narcissistic partner and, when necessary, seeking professional help to navigate the complexities of a marriage affected by narcissistic behaviors.

Overcoming Narcissistic Abuse

6.1   The Healing Process

Healing from narcissistic abuse is a complex and challenging journey, but it is possible with time, effort, and support. The healing process typically involves several stages, including:

> ➤ ***Awareness:*** Recognizing that you are or have been in an abusive relationship with a narcissistic partner is the first step. This awareness can be painful, but it's crucial to acknowledge the problem.

> ➤ ***Education:*** Understanding narcissistic personality disorder and abusive behaviors is important. Knowledge empowers you to make informed decisions and set realistic expectations.

> ➤ ***Self-Care:*** Prioritize self-care to address the emotional and psychological toll of abuse. This may include therapy,

exercise, a healthy diet, and engaging in activities that bring you joy.

➢ **_Setting Goals:_** Establish short- and long-term goals for your recovery. These goals can help you regain a sense of purpose and control in your life.

➢ **_Breaking Ties:_** Reducing or eliminating exposure to the abuser is essential for healing.

➢ **_Rebuilding Self-Esteem:_** Narcissistic abuse often erodes self-esteem. Rebuild your self-worth through self-affirmation, positive self-talk, and self-compassion.

➢ **_Establishing Healthy Relationships:_** As you heal, focus on building healthy relationships with people who respect and support you.

➢ **_Forgiveness:_** Ultimately, forgiveness is about freeing yourself from the emotional burden of the past, not excusing the abuser's actions. It is a personal choice and not a requirement for healing.

6.2 Coping Strategies for Dealing with a Narcissistic Partner

If you are still in a relationship with a narcissistic partner, there are strategies you can employ to protect yourself and improve your well-being.

❖ **_Setting Boundaries_**

Establishing and maintaining boundaries is vital when dealing with a narcissistic partner. This involves:

a) Clearly defining your limits and what behaviors you will not tolerate.

b) Communicating your boundaries assertively but calmly.

c) Enforcing consequences when your boundaries are violated.

❖ *Seeking Therapy and Support*

Therapy and support can be instrumental in coping with a narcissistic partner:

a) Individual therapy can help you process your experiences, build resilience, and develop coping strategies.

b) Support groups provide a safe space to share experiences and gain insights from others who have gone through similar situations.

c) Couples therapy may be an option if your partner is willing to participate, but it can be challenging in cases of narcissistic abuse.

6.3 Why Overcoming Narcissistic Abuse Trauma Takes So Long

Recovering from narcissistic abuse is a process that often takes a significant amount of time. Several factors contribute to the length of this healing journey:

> *Trauma Bonds:* Victims of narcissistic abuse often form strong emotional bonds with their abusers, which can make it difficult to break free.

- ➢ **_Complex PTSD:_** Many survivors of narcissistic abuse develop Complex Post-Traumatic Stress Disorder (C-PTSD), which requires specialized treatment.

- ➢ **_Gaslighting_**: Gaslighting is a manipulative tactic used by narcissists to make their victims doubt their own reality, further complicating the healing process.

- ➢ **_Grief and Loss:_** Healing involves mourning the loss of the idealized relationship you thought you had with the narcissistic partner.

- ➢ **_Rebuilding Trust:_** Trust, both in oneself and in others, can take a long time to rebuild after enduring narcissistic abuse.

- ➢ **_Social Isolation:_** Abusers often isolate their victims, which can leave survivors with a limited support system.

❖ *Cognitive Dissonance*

Victims of narcissistic abuse often experience cognitive dissonance, a state of mental conflict between what they know and the gaslighting or manipulation they experience. Resolving this conflict is a time-consuming process.

❖ *Healing Requires Self-Work*

Healing from narcissistic abuse involves self-reflection, self-awareness, and personal growth. These are not quick fixes and require time and effort.

Overcoming narcissistic abuse is a highly personal journey, and there is no fixed timeline for healing. Seek professional help, lean on your support network, and be patient with yourself as you work towards a healthier, happier life.

Reflection and Conclusion

As you reach the end of this journey through the intricate landscape of marriage, take a moment to reflect on the path you've traveled and the wisdom you've gained. Marriage, in all its beauty and complexity, is a divine union, a bond blessed by God, where two souls come together to create something greater than themselves. It is a journey filled with profound purpose and an ever-evolving commitment to one another.

❖ Reflecting on Your Marriage

In this book, we've explored the foundations of a healthy marriage, from understanding the divine nature of this union to nurturing intimacy in relationships and fostering strong parent-child bonds. These are the building blocks that form the bedrock of a successful and fulfilling marriage. Take a moment to reflect on how these principles have impacted your own marriage and how you can continue to strengthen these foundations.

❖ Key Insights and Lessons

Throughout these pages, we've delved into the recognition and addressing of relationship struggles, including the challenging topic of narcissism in marriage. The insight gained from understanding these struggles is crucial for navigating the storms that may arise in your marriage. What are the key takeaways you've learned about identifying common issues, recognizing narcissistic behaviors, and overcoming narcissistic abuse? How can you apply this knowledge to your own marriage to ensure it remains strong and resilient?

❖ Final Thoughts and Takeaways

In concluding this book, it's essential to remember that marriage is an ongoing journey, a work in progress. No marriage is perfect, and challenges will undoubtedly arise. However, with the knowledge, insight, and strategies you've acquired, you are better equipped to face these challenges with courage, compassion, and resilience. The love and commitment you share with your partner are the cornerstones of your marriage, and they will guide you through even the toughest of times.

In your journey to understanding, strengthening, and sustaining your marriage, always remember that it's the connection between your hearts, the bridge you've built and continue to build, that truly matters. This bridge is nurtured by love, trust, communication, and unwavering support. As you continue to walk this path together, may your hearts remain connected, and your love for one another grow stronger with each passing day.

Author Bio

Grace Akinpetide, Ph.D., MABTS, renowned for her insightful contributions to children's literature, now extends her expertise to the realm of nonfiction with "Bridging Hearts: Understanding, Strengthening, and Sustaining a Marriage." Grace, a scholar with a rich educational background including a Ph.D., DNP, APRN, PMHNP-BC, FNP-BC, and MABTS, ventures into the complexities of marital relationships with the same dedication and empathy that marked her children's stories.

In "Bridging Hearts," Grace applies her understanding of human psychology and her experiences in counseling to explore the nuanced dynamics of marriage. Her approach to writing is grounded in her deep-seated belief in continuous learning and development, qualities that shine through in her exploration of love, intimacy, and the challenges faced by modern couples. With a blend of academic rigor and compassionate insight, Grace offers readers a guide that is as practical as it is profound.

As a devoted lover of Christ, Grace's faith informs her perspective on marriage, infusing the book with values of empathy, compassion, and understanding. "Bridging Hearts" is more than a guide; it's a journey towards healthier, more fulfilling relationships, guided by Grace's unwavering commitment to nurturing love and understanding in all its forms.

Contact Us:

Dear Readers,

Thank you for reading this book.

Visit my website to explore more, share your thoughts, and stay connected. Your presence in this community means everything to me.

http://graciousreadersworld.com/

References:

7 relationship communication exercises to improve your connection. (2023, June 19). Allo Health. https://www.allohealth.care/healthfeed/sex-education/relationship-communication-exercises

Charm and chemistry: Secrets of how to attract a man. (2023, September 6). The Today Man. https://thetodayman.com/how-to-attract-a-man/

Ego vs trust & respect. (2023, August 6). Private Matrix. https://privatematrix.com/trust-respect/

How past traumas can affect relationships and strategies for healing and growth. (2023, January 26). Richard Martinez | Business Coaching Services. https://www.itsrichardmartinez.com/blog/How-past-traumas-can-affect-relationships-and-strategies-for-healing-and-growth-

McAleenan, D. (2023, September 5). Fostering lasting bonds: The art of cultivating meaningful relationships. Medium. https://drewmcaleenan.medium.com/fostering-lasting-bonds-the-art-of-cultivating-meaningful-relationships-60e94e42d9b8

Message, M. (2023, October 9). Symptoms of narcissistic personality disorder (NPD) and relationship challenges. NewsBreak Original. https://original.newsbreak.com/@mint-message-1599872/3185230929234-symptoms-of-narcissistic-personality-disorder-npd-and-relationship-challenges

SelineShenoy. (2021, September 10). How to spot a narcissist: Red flags to watch out for and ways to cope. The Dream Catcher.

https://thedreamcatch.com/how-to-spot-a-narcissist-red-flags-to-watch-out-for-and-ways-to-cope/

Sentrient. (2022, October 12). Workplace culture is paramount for employee health and wellbeing. Sentrient Blog. https://www.sentrient.com.au/blog/workplace-culture-is-paramount-for-employee-health-and-wellbeing

Trigger warning. (2015, March 2). Home. https://umsu.unimelb.edu.au/news/article/7797/2015-03-02-trigger-warning/

Warrior, E. (2023, September 24). Narcissists: When you are on top, their your best friends. Medium. https://medium.com/@empathicwarrior/narcissists-when-you-are-on-top-their-your-best-friends-185eebe1fd07

Wright, M. (2021, September 12). Three keys to self-love — Holistic and somatic therapy | Berkeley & Richmond. Holistic and Somatic Therapy | Berkeley & Richmond. https://www.lifebydesigntherapy.com/blog/three-keys-to-self-love/9/2021

9 781649 539557